The children were making biscuits.

Mo looked at the recipe.
She put in some butter.

Tilak looked at the recipe.
He put in some sugar.

Rosie looked at the recipe.
She put in some flour.

Then a butterfly came into
the classroom.

Everybody looked at the butterfly.

Sam looked at the butterfly.
He put in some salt.

cooking equipment

Tilak said,
'Let's make butterfly biscuits.'

9

Everybody made butterfly biscuits.

The biscuits were horrible!

Tilak said, 'Let's paint them!'

13

Everybody painted
the butterflies and . . .

the children had a butterfly sale.

Other Sam and Rosie Stories at Stage 3

Home Time
A Book for Jack
Tilak's Tooth
Scat Cat!
Lizzie and the Car Wash
The Greedy Guinea-pig
The Ghost in the Castle

The Butterfly Sale

The children were making biscuits.
Find out what happened.

Stage 3

ISBN 0-602-26063-9

9 780602 260637

GINN

ALL ABOARD

Scat Cat!

Julia Jarman

GINN

Julie Park

Written by Julia Jarman
Illustrated by Julie Park

GINN

This book is copyright and reproduction of the whole or part
without the publisher's written permission is prohibited.

© Julia Jarman 1994
Fourth impression 1996
059601

Set ISBN 0 602 25937 1

Published by Ginn and Company
Prebendal House, Parson's Fee, Aylesbury, Bucks HP20 2QY

Printed in Great Britain by Ebenezer Baylis & Son Ltd
The Trinity Press, Worcester, and London